Then I fall asleep very happy, because the best part of Thursdays is when Papi, Mami, and me are all home together!

Mami and Papi tuck me into bed and read me
funny stories with special sound effects.

"Did you have a fun day with Papi?" she asks.
I smile at Papi and say a big "Yes!"

Mami holds me, and she feels soft, so I stay there for a while.

After my bath, I put on my red pajamas
and Papi makes me chicken soup.
I feel it warm me all the way to my toes.
Yum, yum!

Suddenly, we hear the front door.

click! click!

Yay! I love my bath! I jump in with my big boat,
and everything gets very wet—even Papi.

I look at a book about bunnies.

I take my special beetle for a walk.
It makes a very funny noise when I do.

Buzz
Buzz
Bzz!

Then Papi is calling, "It's five o'clock, Orlando. Bath time!"

After lunch, Papi says he has some important things to do, like wash dishes and sort out some very messy papers on his desk.

While Papi does his work, I put on my pirate hat.

I try on Papi's shoes.

Papi makes really yummy pancakes. I run around singing, "*Super pancakes! Super pancakes!*"

For lunch, I will have cheese sandwiches and a chocolate milk shake. That's what Mami always makes me.

"How about some super, *super* pancakes, Orlando?" Papi says.

After that, we pretend to be lions, but we have to stop because I scare myself.

"Lunchtime, Orlando," says Papi. I wave good-bye to Toby.

"Orlando! Orlando!" someone calls.
It's my friend Toby.

Toby and I take turns kicking
his soccer ball along the grass.

It's really nice. I think that Mami would like this tree, too.

At the park, Papi shows me a special
tree with red and golden leaves.

We stand under it and look up,
and it looks like a sky of stars.

Papi shows me a whole lot of things on the way.

A street full of noisy cars,

Beep!
Beep!

I skip because I *love* adventures.

After Papi puts his drum away, he helps me
with my shoes and we go out for a walk.

I sway a bit like this, and move my arms up
and down like that. Then it gets louder and
faster. I dance around and shake my hips.
I feel much better.

up
and
down

Papi says, "That is why it is called the Magic Drum."

I try not to cry, but I do a little, so Papi pulls out his steel drum and asks, "Would you like to hear a song on the Magic Drum?" I am very curious.

Papi begins to play for me, very quietly and slowly.

rum
da de
dum

I look around to show Mami, but then
I remember that today is Thursday.

WOOSh!

Papi sets up a ramp and helps me ride down
on my tricycle. After three tries, I do it by
myself, and he says, "Well done, Orlando!"

Then I remember that Thursday is the day that Papi stays home with me. I start to feel a little bit better.

We wave good-bye to Mami, and Papi says, "Mami will be back tonight, Orlando. In the meantime, let's play!"

After breakfast, I hand Mami crayons so we can draw together while we sing songs. Maybe after that we can go outside. Mami and I always have fun, even if it's just to go get a cup of warm, frothy milk.

But Mami reminds me, "Orlando, today is Thursday."

Thursday is the day Mami has to be busy in town *all* day. I feel sad. I don't like when she is gone all day.

Then Mami sings out, "*Breakfast* time!"
She makes me my favorite breakfast of eggs still
in their shell with funny faces drawn on them.

When I wake up, Mami and Papi give me my usual morning kisses and cuddles in their big, warm bed.

Orlando on a Thursday

emma Magenta

CANDLEWICK PRESS

For Mum and Dad.

Thank you for being *super* parents and a font of support.

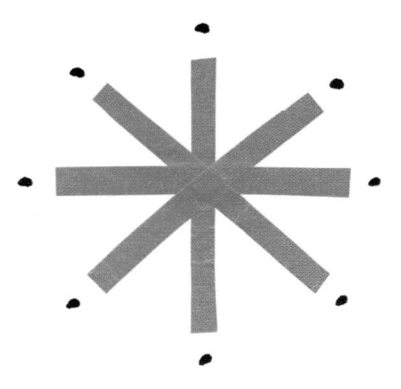

First edition 2010

Library of Congress Cataloging-in-Publication Data

Magenta, Emma.
Orlando on a Thursday / Emma Magenta. — 1st U.S. ed.
p. cm.
Summary: Orlando's Mami is away for the day, but Papi cheers him up by teaching him something new and playing the "Magic Drum" for him.
ISBN 978-0-7636-4560-1
[1. Fathers and sons—Fiction. 2. Bicycles and bicycling—Fiction. 3. Steel drum (Musical instrument)—Fiction. 4. Caribbean Americans—Fiction.] I. Title.
PZ7.M27235Orl 2010
[E]—dc22   2009047406

10 11 12 13 14 15 LEO 10 9 8 7 6 5 4 3 2 1

Printed in Heshan, Guangdong, China

This book was typeset in Avenir Light.
The illustrations were done in collage with found papers, pen, pencil, and Conté crayon.

Candlewick Press
99 Dover Street
Somerville, Massachusetts 02144

visit us at www.candlewick.com

Orlando on a Thursday